Long Ride to Hell's Kitchen

A Jack Cordell Western

R. Annan

Copyright 2015 R. Annan

Edition 1.3

WGA Reg. #: R31397

Printed in the United States of America

Published by One Vision Publishing

e-Book ISBN: 978-1-942338-17-8

Print Book ISBN: 978-1-942338-16-1

Dedication

To a Soldier and a Patriot

SGM Anthony R. Annan, US Army (Ret.)

1.

Hudnell was a quaint little town on the east Kansas plains. The stranger rode slowly in from the west, slumped in the saddle. He had been following the old coach road for three long days. His horse needed a left rear shoe and a rest, and he too was also pretty worn down.

The mid-afternoon autumn air was crisp and fresh but a bit warm for October. The town people were out and about enjoying the change. Some called it Indian summer.

The stranger pulled his black, wide-brimmed hat low and tried to look straight ahead as he followed the road through the middle of town. People stared at him as he passed by. They knew he was an outsider. In Hudnell, everyone knew everyone else.

On the edge of town the stranger found a blacksmith shop with a stable attached. There were several townsfolk standing around talking to the owner. When the stranger stopped they stared at him, watching him dismount, noticing that he wasn't dressed like a cowboy. He wore a suit and the coat hid the handle of his gun. That meant he was either a professional gunslinger or gambler.

"Howdy," the blacksmith said. "What kin I do fer ya?"

"My pal here needs a rear shoe," the stranger said, "and some grub. Can you water him down and scrub him clean? The works."

"My wife is best at thet," the blacksmith said. "She'll fix him up right good."

The stranger smiled and nodded. "Pay now or later?"

"How long you stayin' in town?"

"Overnight, maybe longer. Depends how my luck runs."

"Gambler?" the blacksmith asked. The stranger nodded.

"Come back when ya git ready to leave. Pay then."

"The saddle needs some stichin'."

"The woman kin handle thet, too."

The stranger nodded and reached into his pocket and pulled out an eagle. He put it in the blacksmith's hand. "Give this to her with my compliments, friend," the stranger said.

Before the blacksmith could answer the stranger grabbed his saddlebag and slung it over his left shoulder. He bid the watchers good day and walked stiffly back towards the center of town. It was obvious he had been in the saddle a very long time.

Walking slowly, he nodded politely to the women as be went by. They smiled and nodded back. Gentlemen were rare in Hudnell. The women turned their bonnet-covered heads to follow this attractive looking man. Some giggled and made remarks to their friends. He was good to look at. A fine man.

The cowboys stared at him, as well. Especially those in front of the town saloon. Some chuckled and remarked about his mode of dress, his suit. It was clear to them he was a gambler. They could tell. The way he wore his gun said a lot. He knew how to use it. He didn't flaunt it like some did. He had nothing to prove. He was very confident. They knew they would see him tonight at the gambling parlor.

The stranger was a few yards away from the hotel, when someone shouted, "Jack Cordell!" He flinched for a second, recovered quickly, and walked on.

"Stop, you sidewindin' son of a bitch!"

The stranger turned slowly and stared back down the road. A man dressed in the tight, black clothes of a gunslinger stood with his legs spread in the position of the

3

draw. He wore two pearl handled, single action Colts. His arms were out by his sides, the hands inches from his guns. He was obviously a bounty hunter, out for revenge, or someone with a reputation as a fast gun trying to make a name for himself.

"You've mistaken me for someone else, friend," the stranger said. "I'm not who you think I am."

"You lyin' son of a bitch! Beard or no beard, yer Jack Cordell."

"You're mistaken, my friend," the stranger repeated.

He turned to go and had gone three paces when he heard a gunshot. A bullet kicked up dirt inches from his right boot. He stopped for a moment, sighed, and turned. He put his left hand up to grip his saddlebag.

A crowd began to collect on both sides of the street. People were looking out of shop windows and doorways. A few ran off to tell others what was happening.

The man in black put the gun he had fired back in its holster. He flexed his fingers to limber them up as he looked smilingly at the crowd.

"Folks," the man in black said, "that man there is Jack Cordell, the man who outdrew Red Hardy."

Everyone knew who Hardy was. He was a legendary fast draw artist, a legend in his own time. They also knew that he had been outdrawn by someone called Jack Cordell. But Cordell disappeared the day after he shot Hardy in a poker game, and no one has seen him since. That was five years ago. And here he was now, being braced on Hudnell's main street. It was going to be a historical shoot out.

The crowd studied the two adversaries. One looked every bit like a fast gunslinger, dressed in black from head to toe, with two deadly looking pearl handled Colts. The other man looked more like a card-playing carpetbagger with his back against the wall with nowhere to run, or like a lamb going to the slaughter.

Yet, the stranger stood there relaxed and smiled confidently.

Someone in the crowd yelled out, "He don't look like no Jack Cordell to me! He looks more like a ladies underwear salesman. Haw!" Some of the onlookers guffawed.

"No, he's Cordell," the man in black said. "And he's gonna die right now, right here, in the street of Hudnell!" Then he yelled, "Draw!"

The gunslinger drew both Colts with lightning speed, but somehow something went wrong. His thumbs were still on the hammers when they froze. He suddenly looked confused and surprised. The sun seemed to explode inside his head. His eyes blinked once and went blank as the light in them died. He dropped his guns and sat down in the road. He coughed and fell backwards. He had been shot twice. Once in the chest and once between the eyes. The stranger put his Colt away and walked over to the body.

Someone in the crowd rang out, "Did you see thet?"

"Yeah!" someone answered. "But I don't believe it! Once minute he's just standin' there looking casual like and the next thing he's got his gun in his hand!"

"Gosh! I didn't even see his hand move!"

"Oh, oh! Here comes the Marshal and two deputies!"

"Don't move! You're under arrest, mister!"

The stranger raised his hands and slowly turned to face the Marshal. The two deputies had their Winchesters aimed at his stomach.

"Drop it!"

The stranger nodded and unbuckled his gun belt and let it drop. The Marshal scooped it up. "Let's go," the Marshal said.

The crowd followed behind as the Marshal and deputies took the stranger over to the jail. People moved in from the sides, staring at the stranger, some reaching out to touch him. The deputies pushed them aside, telling them to go home.

The jailhouse was near the stables. It was a small affair built of shale rock and pine with only one large cell. After locking the stranger up the Marshal sat at his desk writing out a report.

2.

Brandon Sawtrell was sixteen when the Mallory Dunn gang murdered his father and did horrible things to his mother and fourteen-year-old sister before killing them.

The Sawtrell family had a small farm west of Coffeeville and the Dunn gang, on the way to rob the Coffeeville Bank, accidently came upon it. When Dunn's four men saw Brandon's mother and sister hanging out the wash in the backyard, they decided to entertain themselves.

The young boy's father was over in the field plowing when he heard the screams. By the time he got on the scene he was exhausted but made a dash into the back of the house, grabbed his shotgun, loaded it, and came out the front. Although he was met with a hail of bullets from Mallory Dunn and his men, he did manage to fire his shotgun as he fell.

At the time this was going on, Brandon was coming out of the woods a half-mile away. He had bagged three rabbits. He felt proud and was anxious to show them to his dad.

He could see the back yard of his house in the distance and heard the echoes of the gunfire. He dropped the rabbits and began to run, watching helplessly as the Dunn gang mounted up and rode off. It seemed like hours before he got to the house. There in the yard, lay the bodies of his mother and sister. In the distance, on the road, he saw the killers riding away like the wind.

The boy got two sheets off the clothesline. They were still damp. Dazed and confused, he covered the bodies of his mother and sister. Reality hadn't set in yet so he wasn't crying.

The sound of a groan made him turn to the edge of the lawn where a cowboy lay holding his stomach. He had been hit by a shotgun blast mid-way. The boy went and stood over him.

"The bastards went and left me," the man whispered. Blood dribbled from the corner of his mouth.

"Who were they?" the boy asked.

"Give me a drink, will ya, kid?"

Brandon went over to the cistern and pumped water into a tin cup and gave it to the outlaw.

"Yer dad. Lucky shot."

"Who were they?"

"Whatta ya wanna' know fer?

"I'm gonna' kill them."

"Yer dad already killed me!" The outlaw tried to chuckle. "He gut-busted me." He coughed up blood. "Damn. It hurts like hell!"

"Who were they, mister?" the boy asked again.

"If you promise to put one in my head, kid, I'll tell ya." He pointed to the boy's .22 caliber rifle. The boy nodded. "It were the Mallory Dunn gang. You ever heard of us?"

"Yeah, everybody's heard of you guys. The Marshal's got yer pictures on the wall of the jailhouse."

"Yeah, that's us, alright. Now, do it kid, do what you promised."

"Brandon!"

The boy heard a gasping voice and turned towards the house.

"Dad!" He ran over to the bloody mess sprawled in the doorway. His father's body was riddled with bullets, as if the

Dunn gang had used him for target practice. He knelt and cried.

"Oh, dad!" he said again, sobbing.

His father's lips moved in a low whisper. The boy bent over to listen. He could barely make out the words as his father kept repeating them over and over, until he could speak no more.

"Kill them all son."

His father sighed and went limp, his open eyes staring blankly at the boy.

"I will, dad. I promise. I swear."

Five years later he would find and kill his first Dunn man in a bar in Hudnell.

The Marshal promptly threw him in jail.

3.

The woman now known as Mrs. Risdale had been married before. Four times, to be exact, and each time she left a grave marker behind. Her surnames had been Oldring, Bishop, Larkin, and Dyer. Her first name was Vera, and she had a daughter named Grace, the result of her first marriage. She and her daughter were both eye-turners, beautiful and refined. Now she was the wife of His Honor, Judge Arnold Risdale, Circuit Court Judge of Bucknel County, Kansas.

The judge, in his early seventies, and she in her mid-forties, made a smart couple. She loved to throw parties, attend social functions, and political rallies, which is where the Judge first met her. He was running for his fourth term and she appeared out of nowhere to work tirelessly to get him re-elected. His wife, in fine health, suddenly died of unknown causes during the campaign. They had no children. A year later he fell in love with and married a woman half his age, Vera Dyer. She became his constant companion after his wife's demise. No one was surprised. She was totally dedicated to the Judge.

Vera Risdale was the happiest woman in the world. She was finally right where she wanted to be, the wife of a wealthy, respected man of importance. She now had status and she and her daughter were secure and respected. Life was just perfect.

Of course there were times when she could have had an occasional clandestine side affair, but those days were over. She learned from experience and decided that this was the life meant for her. She would make it last.

Aside from being the Judge's wife, there was the task of overseeing Grace's life to keep away the schemers and charmers who would come after the beautiful young girl. Vera Risdale took this job seriously and quickly disposed of the more obnoxious suitors in devious ways. Some suddenly and mysteriously developed un-curable symptoms. Some even died. Others merely disappeared only to have their bodies found in a nearby lake or stream.

Of course there was never a clue pointing in Vera Risdale's direction although there were some suitors who became leery and decided it best to keep their distance. If the Judge's wife so much as hinted her displeasure towards them, they found interests in life other than Grace.

As for the good Judge himself, Vera kept a watchful eye on him, making sure he ate properly, cut down on his cigar smoking, and kept civil hours. She also made sure none of his clerks got too close to Grace.

And, if her past should ever catch up with her, what better refuge than being the wife of an influential Judge?

4.

The stranger was asleep on his cot when the Marshal and his deputies came with the kid. They unlocked the cell door and shoved him in. The stranger saw they had roughed him up pretty bad. His face was bruised and his lip was split.

The stranger sat up and stared. "What happened?"

The kid shrugged. "We had a difference of opinion. What's it to ya'?"

"It looks like they won," the stranger said. He got out the fixings and rolled a cigarette.

"Yeah, for now," the kid said. Then, "What kind of crazy town is this?"

"I was wondering the same thing myself, friend. They don't allow for much."

"So I noticed."

They watched the Marshal sit down at his desk and start some paperwork. He began writing fast, not looking up, intent on his work.

"What's he doin'?" the kid asked.

"He's writing up an incident report on you, same as he did on me."

"Incident report? What'll it say?"

"It'll say you're guilty as charged. What did you do?"

"I shot a member of the Mallory Dunn gang. Kilt him daid, the bastard."

"You must be fast, kid." The young man shrugged.

Suddenly the Marshal got up and walked slowly over to them. He stared into the cell for a moment then cleared his throat. "In case you're wonderin' what's gonna' happen, it's this. On Friday, when the stage from Wichita comes in, you two will be put on it and sent west to Bucknel for trial."

"How come Bucknel?" the kid asked defensively.

"How come? Well, the Circuit Judge, Judge Risdale, can't come here on account he's a cripple in a wheel chair. So we usually send cases like you two over there for trial."

"What about witnesses?" the kid said.

"I'm a takin' statements from six witnesses who say they saw what happened," the Marshal said. "All of 'em are upstandin' citizens of Hudnell."

"Is that legal?" the kid persisted.

"It is if those witnesses is certified by me an' my deputies," the Marshal insisted.

"It sure don't sound legal to me."

"It is as long as the Judge allows it," the Marshal said. "If you don't like it, take it up with the Judge, not me."

"Well, I might just do thet," the kid said.

The Marshal went back to his desk and collected his papers and left.

"Where's he goin'?" the kid asked the deputy.

"Over to the saloon."

"What's over there?"

"That's where the witnesses are," the deputy said, chuckling, as if he had told a funny joke.

"The saloon? Yer pullin' my leg!"

"Nope!" the deputy bit a chew from a cud of tobacco. "That's where he always does it, after a few drinks first."

The young man began to pace the cell.

"Relax, kid," the stranger said.

"I can't stay in jail! I promised my paw! I gotta kill a few more a Dunn's men!"

The stranger looked at the young man with a sympathetic eye. "What did they do to you, kid?"

"They kilt my whole family, thet's what."

The stranger whistled. "Sorry about that, kid." Then, "You ever met Mallory Dunn?"

"No, but I'm a lookin' to do just thet."

"Kid, he's poison and fast with a gun, and he always has two backups. You'll never catch him alone."

The kid didn't answer. He sat on a cot and put his hands in his head.

5.

On Friday morning, after a quick cup of cold stale coffee and a piece of hard bread the stranger and the kid were handcuffed and taken over to the stage depot. The deputy in charge carried a packet containing all the witnesses' statements, as well as the Marshal's report and recommendations.

As they stood there next to a bench on a clear, crisp morning, the kid stared at the deputy. "You know I'm bein' framed, don't you?"

"It looks like it, don't it," the deputy chuckled.

"What the hell kind of town are you running here?"

"It ain't my town, sonny-boy, it's the Marshal's. Talk to him about it."

"You crooked son of a bitch!" the kid blurted out.

The deputy drove his fist into the kid's stomach, knocking the wind out of him. He shoved him hard down on the bench. "Now sit and don't make a peep or I'll break your nose!" The kid nodded, gasping for air.

At that moment they heard the pounding of horses coming from the east. A few moments later the six-horse team came to a halt in a cloud of dust. The driver waited for it to settle before he and his shot-gun-toting assistant got down to open the coach door and pull down the folding steps.

"Half-hour layover in Hudnell, Folks! Watch yer steps a gettin' down!"

The first to get out was a short, stocky, bald-headed man with a carpetbag. After him came a clergyman in black, then a seedy looking cowboy with his hat pulled down over his face. He kept his eyes on the ground, and didn't come into the stage depot.

The last to get off were a woman and young girl, both wearing expensive looking bonnets and dresses. They hurried into the shade of the depot and looked around.

"You kin freshen up in there, Mrs. Risdale," the driver said, pointing to a sign that said, 'Ladies'. The two went quickly in out of sight, but not before the stranger caught a glimpse of ruby lips and blue eyes as Mrs. Risdale gave him a quick glance before disappearing.

When they heard the name, Risdale, the two prisoners looked at each other in surprise. The deputy didn't catch it. His mind was somewhere else.

The seedy looking cowboy glanced into the depot then leaned against the stage. He rolled a cigarette and lit it.

"Keep your eye on that one, deputy." The stranger said. "He's up to no good, believe me."

The deputy sneered. "Yeah, like you know," he said. "You never even seen him before, mister."

"I'm telling you, he's up to no good. This stage is gonna get hit and hard."

"Yeah? Well, by who?"

"The Mallory Dunn gang, fellah! I heard they're into robbing stages now, instead of banks."

The deputy thought that over for a moment. He stared through the depot door at the cowboy and noticed he was wearing two guns. The stranger could see the deputy's mind working. He suddenly looked unsure of himself.

Suddenly another deputy came into the depot building carrying a length of light-duty chain in one hand and a lock and key in the other. He spoke to the driver and his shotgun man. The driver took the chain and lock. The deputy called to the other deputy to come along.

"Come on, Pete," he yelled, "we gotta ride! There's trouble at the Bar T."

"What about these two?"

"The driver is gonna chain 'em in!"

The stranger looked over at the driver and the shotgun. He noticed the driver was wearing a gun and was holding the chains up and nodding to him, smiling as he did so.

"Come on, kid," the stranger said.

The two deputies left on the run. The stranger and the kid climbed into the coach. The shotgun covered them as the driver chained them to the U-bolts used to transport prisoners or gold shipments. There was just enough slack to let them sit in the center of the seat.

Twenty minutes later the driver called the passengers back. Once they were settled in, he and the shotgun got up into place. They were soon heading west for Bucknel.

The woman, girl, clergyman, and carpetbagger sat facing the cowboy and two chained prisoners. The coach lurched and bounced as they went along at a slow speed. It was breezy and cool as the October wind cut in through the open windows.

The young girl looked at the cowboy and asked, "What did they do, deputy?"

The cowboy chuckled. "I ain't no deputy, ma'am, and I don't know."

"Oh," the girl said.

"I kilt a man," the kid said. "Shot him daid, ma'am."

"Oh, how awful!"

Vera Risdale stared at the stranger. "And you, sir?"

"The same, ma'am," the stranger said. Their eyes locked for a moment.

"You're both going to hell, you sinners," the clergyman said. "Down on your knees and ask the Lord's forgiveness!"

"Forgiveness for what," the kid said. "Fer lettin' the Dunn gang kill my paw 'n rape 'n murder my little sister and momma? I will like hell!"

"They did that?" Grace Risdale asked sympathetically.

"Yep, and I swore to my dyin' paw I git 'em all."

"Really?"

"Yep, I swore I'd find and kill every stinkin' one of them dirty skunks, if you'll pardon my language, ma'am."

Vera Risdale smiled at the young man with respect for a moment then went stone faced. The stranger saw that and said, "I take it your name is Risdale? The Judge's daughter?"

Vera Risdale laughed. "Dear me no, his wife. And this is my daughter, sir."

The cowboy looked at the stranger. "Judge Risdale is known as the Hangin' Judge. I didn't know if you knew thet."

Vera Risdale gave the stranger a look as if to say, "I'm sorry, but it is true, very true."

After that, they rode on in silence.

6.

Talking wasn't easy because of the loud noise of the pounding horses and the clattering of wheels on the hard packed road. The wind howled inside the coach. After two hours they stopped at a crossroad and the cowboy got out. The shotgun handed him down his saddle and worn out Winchester and he walked off to the left, heading south. The stage continued west towards Bucknel.

The kid kept staring at young Grace Risdale. She saw this and got a book from her bag and pretended to read.

"It'll be a pleasure to have the father of the prettiest girl in the world hang me, ma'am," the kid suddenly blurted out. Grace Risdale started to giggle.

Vera Risdale smiled and said, "Judge Risdale doesn't actually hang people himself, young sir. He has other people to that." Then, looking at the stranger, "The Judge is not Grace's father, he's her stepfather." The stranger wondered why she had offered this information to complete strangers. She stared at him intensely when she said it.

The stranger gave the chains a sudden yank to test the U-bolt. It held firm. He shrugged and smiled.

The stagecoach came to a long uphill climb and began to slow down a bit, but once on the backside the driver had to work the brakes so the coach wouldn't override the horses. At the bottom the land leveled out and the ride was smoother for miles on.

They stopped in the afternoon at a cluster of buildings alongside the road for another rest. There was a saddler's place and a shop that repaired guns and rifles. In the back, in a clearing were several sod homes and a church. The little carpetbagger and the clergyman got out there. After half an hour the stage left, but not before the driver checked to make sure the prisoner's chains were secure.

Vera Risdale stared at the stranger. "My husband is really a very good Judge, you know."

"I'm sure he is, ma'am," the stranger responded. Then, "But do you think he should hang this boy for defending his family?"

"I'm sorry but he took the law into his own hands."

The stranger shrugged. "Wouldn't you?"

"Well, I suppose so."

"Thanks for being honest, ma'am."

"And you, sir, do you have a family?"

"No."

"Oh, no one? A sweetheart, perhaps?"

"None at the moment, ma'am."

"You're a gambler, aren't you?"

The stranger chuckled. "You guessed that right, lady. I am a gambler by trade."

"It's a shame to see a fine looking man like you in this situation," she said. "I feel sorry for you."

"Believe me ma'am I feel a lot sorrier than you do."

Vera Risdale was just about to answer when they heard a volley of gunshots coming from the road up ahead. The driver shouted, "Outlaws!" and jammed on the brakes so hard those inside could smell wood scorching. The coach shuddered and came to a stop.

They heard the shotgun go off above them. It was answered by two rifle shots. The shotgun man spiraled to the ground. There was a brief exchange between the driver and the outlaws and he tumbled down, hit the road, and rolled away into the grass.

They heard horses pounding in close, coming up to the coach. Men were heard dismounting and talking. Some were laughing. Seconds later two men wearing bandanas stared into the coach. Mrs. Risdale stiffened up and looked at them sternly.

"How dare you! Do you know who I am, sir?"

"Of course we do, ma'am!" one of the masked men said. "You're the wife of Hangin' Judge Rizzy! Haw!" Then, "And we're here to fetch you!"

Vera Risdale reached quickly into her purse and pulled out an over and under derringer. She shot a hole in the bandit's head. He disappeared from sight.

Grace Risdale screamed and fainted.

7.

"She kilt Turk!" the other outlaw yelled out. He ducked just as Vera Risdale fired the second barrel of her little derringer at his face. She missed. She threw the weapon at him. Her aim was true this time, and it hit him in the eye. He jumped down from the coach, crying in pain.

Both doors of the coach were thrown open and four outlaws tried to cram their bodies through at once. One pulled Vera out onto the road screaming and kicking. Another carried the unconscious Grace in his arms.

A huge man climbed laboriously up into the coach. He was wearing crossed gun belts hidden in front by his overhanging belly. He had stubby legs and a neck as thick as a pig's mid-section. His face was covered by a red bandana, but it was plain to see he had twinkling, dancing, grey-green, sad eyes.

"I'm Croak Cantrell," he said in a deep rusty voice. "It looks like you two fellahs got yerselfs in sort of a bind."

He laughed and his bulging stomach shook like half a tub of melted lard.

"Hey, looky here, men! I'd say we got ourselves a couple of jailbirds. Haw!"

A dozen heads poked in through the narrow coach door openings. A roar of laughter cut the air, followed by crude remarks. The outlaws were enjoying the sight of two of their own in chains.

"The driver has all the keys," the stranger said.

"Oh, does he now? And what's thet to me, friend?"

"How about a little professional curtesy, one crook to another?"

The big bull of a man roared with laughter. The coach shook.

"Listen to him, men," he yelled out. "He thinks were in the same game! Haw!" Then, soberly, "Give me one good reason we should cut you two loose, mister."

"Ah, right now I can't think of any, to be truthful," the stranger said.

Someone yelled into the coach. "Bring 'em out! Let's see what they're made of!"

The leader thought about that for a moment, then growled, "Okay, but make it snappy. We can't stay here all day."

"Kin I see yer face, mister?" The kid asked.

The outlaw nodded. "Sure, why not, kid. One way or the other, you won't be alive to tell about it anyway.

The bandit pulled his bandana down around his thick neck to reveal a face with a huge, bulbous nose and sausage-like lips. The kid stared intensely at him.

"Satisfied, kid?"

"Yes, sir. Thank you sir," the kid said. He looked disappointed.

"Well, don't cry, sonny-boy," Croak Cantrell said. "I ain't gonna hurt ya. But my men might." He broke out laughing again.

One of the outlaws came with the keys and unlocked the chain and the handcuffs. The prisoners had cuff burns on their wrists. They shook their aching arms to get the blood flowing.

"Let's go, amigos," the outlaw leader said.

"Why don't you just leave us and go on?" the stranger asked.

The outlaw chuckled. "Oh, no, that wouldn't be any fun, now would it?" He drew his gun and motioned for the two to get out. "Vamoose! We're gonna play a little game of quick draw." The stranger suddenly smiled. "You might not be smilin' in a few minutes, slick."

"Would you like to lay a few double eagles on it, my friend?" the stranger said. "Just to make it interesting?"

The old outlaw chuckled. "Why sure, how many is interestin'?"

"Fifty?"

"Whew! You sure dream big, mister, I'll admit ta thet! Okay, fifty it is." Then, "I trust you have fifty, friend?"

"The lady will cover me," the stranger said, smiling confidently.

"Okay, let's do it."

The stranger and the kid followed the big outlaw chief out onto the road. The outlaw looked around then pointed to the dead driver and the shotgun man.

"Git their gun belts and give 'em to these two innocents," he said with a sneer. In a moment the kid and the stranger were strapping them on. The stranger checked and reloaded the cylinder.

The kid looked at the stranger. "My name is Brandon Sawtrell. I'm a farmer. My family had a small farm near Wichita."

The stranger smiled and nodded. "Then I'll call you Wichita, if you don't mind, kid? I'm called Brazos."

The two women stood watching. Grace Risdale clung to her mother, sobbing. Vera Risdale stared hard at the stranger, fascinated. "They're going to be murdered, mother," Grace cried. Her mother didn't seem to hear. Her eyes were on the stranger.

"Tully! Baily!" the outlaw leader called out. "Over in thet field!" He pointed to a large, level, grassy spot just off the road.

The two designated gunmen walked casually over into the field and got into position at one end.

"They the fasted you got?" the stranger asked. The outlaw chief nodded.

"They're greased lighnin'."

But the stranger had already started off at a fast walk. He reached the field way ahead of the kid and faced the two outlaws. They were arguing.

"I want him, Tully! You had the last one!"

"Screw you, Baily! He's mine! I'm gonna gut shoot the bastard!"

"That ain't fair, Tully! Let me have this one!"

"How about we both go for it. See who hits him first?"

"Well, okay then."

The stranger stood a moment smiling, then shouted out, "Draw!"

Everyone on the road heard the shout and stared on in awe as Tully and Baily went for their guns, then stopped as if frozen. There were two shots and the stranger's gun was already out and spitting smoke. No one ever saw him draw. Tully and Baily looked at each other in surprise and fell in a heap, firing their guns into the ground.

By then the stranger had already reloaded and was walking back to the road. He met the kid halfway and winked at him. The boy looked relieved.

"Damn," the kid said. The stranger chuckled. The two walked back to the road together.

The outlaws were dead quiet. Finally Croak Cantrell said, "Who the hell are you, mister?"

"They call me Brazos," the stranger said. Then, "What's the deal with the women? Is this a kidnapping?"

"More of a swap," Croak said. "They got my gal in the Bucknel jail and they're gonna hang her."

The stranger nodded. "How you gonna pull that off?"

"I'm not sure, yet." Then, "Right now we better ride before somebody comes along an' we'll have to kill 'em."

"You're not letting the kid and me go, then, I take it?"

"Not now, maybe later on. I gotta think about it more. I'd like ta get your notions on how we kin do this thing. Do ya mind?"

The stranger chuckled. "No, seeing as you have all the guns here." He looked at the women. Vera Risdale was still staring at him with those inviting blue eyes. She knew he was her only shield from harm. "How about giving the women some respect?"

"Sure," Croak said. "I kin do thet."

While the women, the stranger, the kid, and Croak Cantrell got back in the coach, the bodies of the dead driver and shotgun were laid near the road. The two dead outlaws were loaded on top of the coach. The passengers were blindfolded.

"Where are we going?" the stranger asked.

"To a little place of mine called Hell's Kitchen," Croak said. "I think you'll kinda like it." He let out a raspy chuckle.

The stage started moving out.

8.

Hell's Kitchen was an elusive place Kansas lawmen longed to find. They searched and searched for it until they began to think that it didn't really exist. Maybe it was just a made-up name to keep lawmen busy and off the trails of real outlaws.

It was rumored that Hell's Kitchen was where the old outlaw gangs went to retire and enjoy a life of leisure, spending their ill-gotten gains on whiskey, women, and cards. It was said outlaws like Daggs Everett, Frost Winslow, Scotty Randal, and Joel McCready went there to avoid the bounty hunters and lawmen. It was like a waiting room for rustlers, train and bank robbers, and other scoundrels to abide their time and die in peace.

Croak Cantrell had been out of service for several years. Things had gotten too hot for him and his men after the botched Cattlemen's Trust job. Five of his men were shot to ribbons by the new Marshal there in Cheneyville, but those that came through did manage to get half a million dollars.

They took the money and built a secure hideaway where they would never be found, deep in the hills and pine forests.

It was as if they had vanished from the face of the earth.

With an outlaw driving, the coach clattered west on the road for several miles then turned right into a ridge of trees. In a moment it got darker and cooler. They could smell the scent of pine trees. The coach slowed down and the wheels made very little noise on the pine needle-cover ground. It made many turns left and right, and the ground swerved up and down again and again. It was almost like being in a boat at sea. Those inside had to brace themselves at each twist and turn.

"What is going to happen to my daughter and me, sir?"

"That depends on yer husband, ma'am."

"What do you want from him, Mr. Cantrell?"

"I'd like to swap you and your little girl here for my baby-doll, Squirrel-tooth Mary, is what I'm aimin' ta do, ma'am."

At the name Squirrel-tooth Mary, Mrs. Risdale suppressed the urge to laugh. "What was her crime, sir?"

"The damn fool ran off with a Mallory Dunn man, and tried to rob the Hudnell Bank."

"Just the two of them? That wasn't very smart," Mrs. Risdale said.

The kid cleared his throat. "Did you say the Mallory Dunn gang?"

"Yep, 'n they got caught. The Marshal sent them to Bucknel to be tried and hung."

"Do you know the Dunn gang?" the kid asked.

"Shucks, yeah! They came in two months ago. He's been hidin' at Hell's Kitchen ever since! You know him?"

"Sort of. His gang kilt my whole family five years ago just fer the fun of it! I swore to get every last sidewinder in his gang!"

Croak Cantrell chuckled. "Well thet should be fun ta see, kid. There's six of them left. You gonna take 'em all by yerself?"

"It don't make a hill of beans to me how many they is, Mr. Cantrell," the kid said. "I'll kill 'em or die tryin'!"

"That'll most likely be the outcome, kid. You pushin' up daisies. Maybe you'd best think about it before you jump."

They listened to the outside sounds for a moment.

They could feel and smell the musty coolness and dampness of the forest as they went deeper in. Crows were cawing and flying somewhere above them. It felt as if they had negotiated a vast, endless natural labyrinth.

"You, young sir?" Grace Risdale said.

"Wichita, ma'am," the kid answered. "Call me Wichita, if you would."

"Isn't your friend going to help you on your quest for revenge?"

She heard him say, "You'd best ask him, ma'am."

"Sir, are you going to assist your friend, Mr. Wichita?"

"We're not really friends. We just met in jail a short while ago, ma'am."

"But he can't possibly ---"

"Be quiet, Grace!" her mother said sharply. "They're just stupid cowboys. That's what they do, shoot each other."

"Yes, mother." Grace Risdale fell quiet No one spoke after that.

In another hour the land tilted downward and the horses' hooves rang out on the rocky incline. Pine branches rubbed against the sides of the coach. As they descended in a straight line, they were told to remove their blindfolds. They saw that they were entering a narrow chokepoint that cut through a rock wall. There was a guard shack there and two armed guards. They waved at the outlaws as they filed through. It was just wide enough to let the coach in.

When the road leveled off they saw cattle roaming freely on the grassy knolls in the distance. The scent of pine smoke was in the air and log cabins began to appear, along with larger clapboard structures with slate shingle roofs.

There was a blacksmith, a stable, a gunsmith shop, and other small businesses around a small lake. It all sat in a small bowl surrounded by cliffs and a thick pine forest. Eagles circled high above.

The coach stopped at the stables and they all got out and stretched their legs. Cantrell's men unloaded the two bodies and took them off to bury them. The outlaw chief waved to the hostages, and led them away.

They walked around the lake to what looked like a two-story lodge built from pine timber. They went up the stairs to the porch and into the lobby. On the left was a dining room and on the right was a bar room. Oil lamps hung from the ceiling rafters in the lobby and both rooms.

"Don't try to leave," the outlaw chief said. "There ain't no way out 'ceptin' through the chokepoint."

Vera Risdale looked around the lobby. "What a disgusting place."

"Well, if yer luck holds out, you won't have to suffer it long," Croak said. "The quicker I get my baby-doll back, the quicker yer outta here."

"What do you want from me, Mr. Cantrell?" Vera asked.

"You write a letter and I'll get it to the Judge. Ifn I git the right answer then everybody'll be happy."

"And if not?"

"Let's not think on thet, ma am," the grizzled, old outlaw said. "At least not yet." Then, "Hey, Bill! You got customers!"

A bent-over, hip-shot old man came out from the back room and walked up to the desk. He stared at the four newcomers and sniffed and wiped his nose on a soiled bandana.

"Bill, these are my special guests. See thet they git the royal treatment," the outlaw said. "And give the ladies the bridal suite." He looked at the kid. "I'll get word to Mallory Dunn thet yer a lookin' fer him, kid. You best practice on yer draw." The outlaw left laughing. It was now dark outside.

9.

Hell's Kitchen hotel had less than bare bones accommodations. Vera Risdale and her daughter were given a rustic room with a large four-poster bed and a single window with frosted glass. It also had a chamber pot and a washstand, but nothing else except a worn rug on the floor.

"This is what we call our luxury suite," old Bill proudly proclaimed as he lit the oil lamp. "And thet there is the luxury bed."

Vera smiled at old Bill and put a soft, warm hand on his bent shoulder. He could smell her expensive perfume, and stared up into her face as if hypnotized.

"William," Vera Risdale said. "May I call you William?"

"Yesum, ma'am!" Bill said.

"Are you a gentleman, William?" Before the old man could answer, she went on. "I do believe you are, sir." She went into a monologue about how grateful she and her daughter would be if he would attend to their special needs.

In the end she handed old Bill a double eagle. When his eyes popped open she knew Bill was a bought man.

Across the hall the stranger and the kid had a smaller room. It had two cots, a washbowl on a stand and a chamber pot. Its window looked out into the street. They lit the oil lamp and sat on their cots talking.

"You got a big problem, kid," the stranger said.

"Mallory Dunn? Yeah, I know."

"Croak will make sure Dunn knows you want to brace him."

"Will he come a lookin'?"

"No, he'll have his men come kill you."

The young man shrugged. "There ain't much I kin do, I guess. I'm about good as dead, I suppose."

"Let me see your Colt," the stranger said.

The kid handed the stranger his gun. The stranger spun opened the cylinder and removed the bullets. He closed the cylinder and aimed the empty Colt at the wall and pulled the trigger s few times. He grimaced.

"What's the matter?" the kid asked.

"What you got here is an old model, kid. It's too slow. You need a faster gun with a filed down tang. One with the front sight taken down so flat it don't catch in the holster."

"I don't know where I kin git one of those, do you?"

"First thing in the morning we'll take a look around town and see." The stranger said. "But right now we'd better get some sleep." He got up and blew out the lamp.

In the morning they went down to the lobby. There was a pine board sign above the dining room entrance that said 'Hell's Kitchun. Food Fit Fer The Devul.' They saw several people getting tin plates, knives, forks, and spoons from a long table where trays of ham, scrambled eggs, bread, and jelly were lined up. There was a large coffee urn at one end. A hat lay at the front of the table with a sign that read 'Breakfast-One Quarter Eagle.'

Going to a far table, they ate with their backs against the wall and their eyes on the doorway. The ladies were nowhere in sight. In twenty minutes the stranger and the kid were out on the street in the early morning light.

"I noticed a gun shop when we came in," the stranger said. It's down the road a ways."

46

As they walked along the muddy street, people stared at them. It seemed like a normal little town, except there were very few women and children. Mostly cowboys and some tradesmen. They kept on going until the stranger pointed off to the left.

"There it is, kid."

They went into the gun shop. It was well stocked. There were several model 1862, .36 caliber Colts and a lot of 1873, .36 caliber versions. There was a Richards-Mason Colt conversion revolver and a Thuer conversion of a model 1861 Naval Revolver.

The owner smiled as he watched their faces. They were like kids in a candy store.

What caught the stranger's eye was a matched pair of Colt .45 caliber, single-action 1874 revolvers. Both had ivory handles and were sleek and clean.

"Can you modify these two? File down the tang and flatten the front sights?" the stranger asked.

"That'll be extra," the owner said through thick glasses.

"How long?"

"About an hour, if the wife helps."

"The stranger nodded and the owner took the guns into the back room.

"I ain't got no money," the kid said.

The stranger sat on a stool and removed his left boot. He reached in and pulled out several flattened bank notes valued at one hundred-dollars each. He handed one to the kid.

"They smell a little, but they still good."

"Wow! I ain't never seen that much before!"

They went next door to the saddlery and bought two saddlebags, then returned to the gun shop. The owner finally came out with the Colts. "Anything else, gentlemen?"

"Eight boxes of ammo," the stranger said.

They lay their old Colts on the counter and shoved the new ones into their holsters.

"Let me see you draw, Wichita," the stranger said.

The kid made several draws. The stranger adjusted his gun belt, bringing the holster higher.

"You don't want the holster too low, kid. It makes for a slow draw. You've got to do it all in one fast motion. Pull thumb and fire, pull thumb and fire. Try it." He watched. "Feel better?"

"Yeah, lots better," the kid said, smiling.

The stranger loaded the cylinders and put the rest of the cartridges into the two saddlebags. He paid the bill and changed a bank note for eagles for him and the kid. They slung their saddlebags over their shoulders and left.

They were a dozen yards down the street when two cowboys called from thirty feet away, on the other side.

"Hey kid! You the dumb clod-hopper whose lookin' fer Mr. Dunn?" People immediately scattered off the street into alleyways and stores.

"Are you Mr. Dunn?" the kid asked.

"Nope. He ain't got time for piss-ants like you, kid, so we're here to take care of the light work."

"I ain't got no quarrel with you," the kid said.

"Yer mother was a slut who worked in a bar," the outlaw yelled across the street at the kid. "Will thet do it?'

"You shouldn't a said thet," the kid yelled back.

"Why? What cha gonna do, cry?"

"No, I guess I'm gonna kill you," the kid said.

The outlaw drew and so did the kid. The outlaw's bullet took the kids hat clean off his head. The kid's shot smacked the outlaw between the eyes, snapping his head back. He dropped his gun. His body danced a little and he collapsed in the mud of the street.

The other outlaw saw that the stranger had beaten him to the draw. He shoved his gun back into his holster and held his hands up.

"I'm fine, mister," he said loudly. "I'm leavin'."

"Not alone," the stranger said. "Take your friend."

The outlaw nodded and hoisted his partner up on his shoulder and struggled away with his burden.

The stranger saw that the kid's gun hand was shaking.

"Scared, Wichita?" The kid nodded. "You'll get used to it." Then, "From now on, don't go for the head. Go for the chest. This time you were lucky."

The stranger picked up the kid's hat and looked at it. He whistled. "That was close, very close." He handed the kid his hat. "You alright?"

"Yeah, I guess." Then, "He shouldn't a said thet about my momma."

The stranger chuckled. "He won't say it any more, kid."

"I don't feel so good. I never do after a killin'."

"It'll pass. Come on let's get back to the hotel before we have to shoot our way back."

They hurried back to the hotel.

10.

Late in the afternoon the kid and the stranger went down to the lobby. Looking into the dining room they saw Vera and Grace Risdale eating at a table by a window. They removed their hats and went in to join them. Mrs. Risdale asked them to sit down.

"What's on the diner menu?" the stranger asked.

"They call it venison stew, Mr. Brazos."

"Any good?"

"It's very salty," Mrs. Risdale said. Then, "Mr. Brazos, could I talk to you?"

"You sure can, ma'am. Ah, what about?"

"About our situation, Grace's and mine."

"What about it?"

"I'm afraid that the Judge will not give in, Mr. Brazos. He's a stubborn old man and holds fixed convictions about the law."

"Wouldn't he allow for this situation?"

52

"No, I'm certain he will not. He won't budge an inch, I'm afraid."

"You're saying he's going to hang Cantrell's woman?"

"Yes her and her accomplice."

"Have you any idea when?"

"Probably at the end of the month. That's when they hold Retribution Day in Bucknel. It's known as Hanging Day."

"That's what, five days from now?"

"Yes, and you know what Mr. Cantrell has in mind for my daughter and I, don't you?"

The stranger nodded. "But maybe it's just talk. He's a big blow-hard, likes to bluster and exaggerate."

"Do you think so?"

"Well, I can't be certain, ma'am."

Suddenly the kid blurted out, "I won't let him hurt you, ma'am! I'll die first."

"That's very brave of you, Wichita, but I'm afraid you'd be killed in the end, anyway, you see."

The stranger looked at Mrs. Risdale. "What do you want me to do?"

"Well, I was hoping you could think of some way to sway Mr. Cantrell's mind. There must be some way out of our situation." She paused and gave the stranger an inviting stare.

"I'd like to, but…"

"I would be very grateful, sir," she said softly, staring into his eyes. "Very, very grateful in all ways." The stranger caught the hidden meaning, the coded invitation.

Grace Risdale was looking adoringly at the kid. His face was turning red.

The stranger cleared his throat to break the spell. He chuckled. Vera Risdale was a man-eater, a web-weaver. And she knew the code of the west. It said: always help the helpless.

"As I said, sir, I am more than willing to show my gratitude," she repeated.

"I'll see what I can do, ma'am," the stranger said. Then, as if struck with an idea, he asked, "Have you seen the jailhouse there in Bucknel?"

"Of course. It's next to the courthouse for convenience. I have visited it with my husband, the Judge, many times."

"Would it be possible for you to draw a sketch or a map of it? The floor plan?"

"Yes, I think so. Why?"

"Excuse me, I'll be right back."

The stranger went into the lobby and shortly returned with a paper and pencil. He handed both to Mrs. Risdale.

"I need a simple floor plan with front and back, if you would, ma'am."

Fifteen minutes later he held a detailed sketch in his hand.

"That rear window? How many bars?"

"Three, I think."

The stranger nodded and folded the paper and stuck it in his pocket.

"Very good, ma'am."

The stranger turned to the kid who had locked eyes with the beautiful young Grace Risdale. She had him lassoed and hog-tied. He couldn't move.

"Let's eat, kid!"

Young Brandon Sawtrell didn't blink an eye.

"Let's eat! Go get some of that venison stew, kid!" He repeated louder. The kid shook off the spell and came back to life.

He and the stranger went over to the serving table and got their food. They sat with their backs to the wall, eating.

Later they found Croak Cantrell in a small, poorly built log cabin near the stables. He was all alone and had been drinking heavily.

"Sit down, fellahs," Cantrell croaked. His baggy eyes were bloodshot.

"Thanks," they said and sat at the table across from the big man.

"Have a drink?"

"Ah, maybe not," the stranger said. "Still trying to digest that venison stew we just had."

"We're tryin' to improve thet," Croak said. "The next time we're gonna grab us a real cook." He chuckled. "So what's up?"

"Did you send off that letter to the Judge yet?"

"No, why?" Croaked asked. He took a pull from a pint of rotgut whiskey.

"No need to send it," the stranger said.

"Why is thet?"

"It wouldn't do any good. The lady said so."

"She did?" Croak said in a thick, whiskey soaked voice.

"Yes, but don't worry, I've got a plan to get your baby-doll back before the Judge hangs her."

"You'd do thet fer old Croak?"

"Sure, if you let us out of here. All of us."

The old outlaw shifted his considerable weight in his chair. He nodded. "Okay. You do thet fer old Croak 'n you and the ladies get an escort outta here." Then, "What's yer plan?"

"Give me three men and the kid and I'll go and bust Squirrel-tooth Mary out of the Bucknel jail. The lady gave me the jail floorplan."

"I suspect you and the kid might be able ta do it with a couple of my boys ta back you up." Then, "It sure would be nice ta see my baby-doll agin. I miss her somethin' bad."

"We'd have to move fast, though," the stranger said. "I figure it's at least three days ride west to Bucknel."

"By golly, it's a deal! Shake on it, friend!" Big Croak Cantrell reached across the table and grabbed the stranger's hand. "I'll give you three of my best men."

"Good."

"I'd like to go with you all, but I got troubles a brewin' right here. If I left, why, they'd take over." Croaked sniffed and wiped his huge nose with his bandana.

"Who?" the stranger sked.

"Mallory Dunn and his boys. He's been stirrin' up trouble ever since he got here. I'm sorry I let the bastard in! He wants ta take over everything I built."

The stranger nodded sympathetically then said, "Have your men meet us at the stables in the morning, at sun-up."

The stranger and the kid left and walked back to the hotel to tell Vera Risdale the plan. She put a hand on his arm and gazed up into his eyes.

"Thank you, sir. If your plan works, you will be rewarded in a way I'm sure you'll enjoy," she said softly.

He felt the firm, telling pressure of her fingers on his gun hand.

11.

There were no blindfolds this time, but even then the tortuous, turning trail out of Hell's Kitchen was like getting out of the bowels of hell. They burned up half a day just to get out of the huge pine forest and onto the road west. Once there they made good time. The stranger and the kid were mounted on two good outlaw horses that could stand long, hard rides.

They stopped once long enough to eat jerky and hard tack. The stranger and the kid had water in their canteens, but the three Cantrell men, Pilchuck, Burns, and Tragg, had whiskey in theirs, as well as a bottle each in their saddlebags.

They made first camp in a stand of aspens far off the road. Right away Pilchuck and Tragg started to argue over something. At first the stranger didn't listen, but when he heard Squirrel-tooth Mary's name, he took an interest.

"I'm tellin' you Tragg," Pilchuck said, "It's her an' Dunn's man, Sprague!"

"Yer full of it, Pilchuck," Tragg said. "Ain't he full of it, Burns? Tell 'em! He's full if it!"

"Hell, I don't know," Burns said. "Maybe he is 'n maybe he ain't."

"I'm tellin' ya, Tragg, I seen 'em one night. Old Croak was dead drunk. I happened by the cabin an' I seen them a kissin'. Mary and Sprague!"

"No ya didn't, Pilchuck," Tragg said. "You never did!"

"I swear! Then they went into the back room where the bed is. I watched for over an hour an' finally Sprague, well, he come out alone lookin' all worn out 'n tired."

"Yeah? Well, what then?"

"Nothin', he jest left!"

"Well, you shoulda plugged him good, Pilchuck," Tragg said. "I woulda."

The stranger looked over at the kid. The kid nodded. It seemed that Squirrel-tooth Mary and Dunn's man, Sprague were lovers. They had run off together to rob the Hudnell bank and got caught.

In the morning, while the others were out of earshot, the kid said, "Did you get all that last night about Squirrel-tooth Mary and Dunn's man, Sprague?"

"Yeah, I did."

"What'll we do?"

"Nothing. It doesn't change anything. Let Croak deal with it. Maybe he knows and wants to get his hands on the two of them."

"So you think when we bring them back, Mr. Cantrell will kill them both?"

"It's not our problem, kid," the stranger said. "All we have to do is bring them back and we get to get out of Hell's Kitchen."

"Yeah, I guess so." The kid shrugged.

The weather was fine and they made good time. On the third day they reached the outskirts of Bucknel. They pulled back a mile and found a place to hide in a stand of scrub oaks.

The three outlaws laid low while the stranger and the kid went to check the jail out. The town was getting ready for Retribution Day. A gallows stood in a courtyard in front of the jail alongside the courthouse, and a podium was nearby for politicians to make speeches on. A banner hung above the courthouse door.

"Looks like the Judge is running for re-election," the kid chuckled. His name was on the banner.

Since it was a Saturday, the day before the hangings, there wasn't much going on in Bucknel. It looked like any other sleepy western town with picnics in the park and a band playing in the square.

There was an old abandoned building across the street directly in front of the jailhouse. Its roof had caved in and its clapboard walls were crumbling. They rode past it once, then came around behind it and stopped.

"Mrs. Risdale said this use to be a library."

"It's seen its days," the kid said.

"This is where you and Pilchuck will come. You'll fire over into the jailhouse to keep the guards busy so the rest of us can do our job." The kid nodded. "But be careful because they'll fire back."

"This is gonna be a tight squeeze."

"Yeah, very tight."

The kid and the stranger dismounted and walked casually over to the courthouse. It was closed. They walked around the back and kept going until they were behind the jailhouse. The stranger stood there rolling a cigarette fifteen feet in front of the window. A deputy rode slowly by. He glanced at them and stopped.

"Good-day, Deputy," the stranger said. "Lovely weather for a hanging, I'd say." He lit his cigarette.

The deputy chuckled. "Is that what you'd say?"

"Yes, sir, that's just what I'd say, Deputy."

The deputy chuckled again and rode out of sight. The stranger walked over to the window. He tossed the lit cigarette in past the bars.

"Hey!" someone yelled. A man's face appeared behind the bars. "What the hell you want, fellah?"

"I'd like to talk to the girl."

Someone shoved the man aside. A young slightly bucktoothed face replaced the man's. It had blue eyes and short, curly, auburn hair and was very pretty.

"What the hell you want, handsome?"

"I want you, baby-doll," the stranger said smiling.

"Then come 'n git me, mister," Mary purred. "I'm a waitin' 'n a wantin'! I'm hot to trot, gorgeous!"

"I'll be back tonight."

"No foolin'? Fer real?"

"Be ready to ride, sweetheart," the stranger said.

"Yer crazy as hell, mister," Mary said. "But I'm game ifn you are." Then, "Who's that cute one you got with you? Is he yer pard?"

"Yep, he's my pard." Then, "See you later."

The stranger and the kid walked away.

"She's a pretty little pixie, ain't she? I kin see why Croak is all in a tither over her," the kid said.

"Yep," the stranger said. "She's the kind of woman outlaws kill over."

They walked back to their horses.

12.

About two o'clock on Sunday morning they snuck silently into the town of Bucknel and took up their positions. There was no moon. Bucknel seemed like a deserted ghost town. A dog barked down by the stables. Suddenly they heard distant gunfire out front and knew that the kid and Pilchuck had started as planned.

They heard a guard inside the jail yell and another joined in as they scrambled around in the dark to get their rifles and return fire.

The stranger, Burns, and Tragg walked their horses up to the jailhouse window, tied ropes around the bars, and nudged their horses. The bars and a large portion of the jailhouse's rear fieldstone wall fell down.

Squirrel-tooth Mary was the first to come running out. The stranger scooped her up on the cantle. She fitted in neatly behind him and wrapped her arms around his waist and hung on tightly.

"What about Sprague?" she asked.

"They'll bring him," the stranger yelled as they went crashing out of town.

"Who the hell are you, darlin'?" she asked.

"Let's just say I'm an admirer of yours, sweetheart!"

"Yer plumb crazy, mister!"

They rode on. Low clouds began to form overhead and the night turned blacker than coal. It grew cooler and the wind lashed at them. They could hear hoof beats far behind, getting closer, but no gunfire. By dawn they would have a good lead on the posse.

At sun up they stopped to wait for the others. The kid, Pilchuck, Burns, and Tragg finally came up. They all dismounted and drank.

"Where's Sprague?" Squirrel-tooth Mary asked. She looked angry. "One of you were supposed to bring him!"

"He's dead," Tragg said. "A deputy shot him in the back. I had to dump him."

"What? You dumped him?"

"I had ta, he was daid," Tragg said.

"You lying bastard," Mary screamed. She rushed Tragg, her arms flailing. Her fingernails raked his face. "You kilt 'em!"

Tragg finally pushed her off. "So what? What's he to you, baby-doll? Haw!"

Squirrel-Toothed Mary shrugged. She sighed and backed over towards Burns. She grabbed the gun out of his holster and fanned it like a man. She shot Tragg in the chest three times just as he reached for his gun. She turned the barrel on Burns.

"Now, wait a minute baby-doll! I didn't do nothin'!" Mary emptied the cylinder into Burn's belly.

"You sons-a-bitches! You know we never leave no one behind! Thet's the rule!" Mary screamed, dropping the gun. She began to shake and sob.

"We have to leave," the stranger said.

Mary stripped off both Tragg's and Burn's gun belts and strapped them on. They seemed too large for her small frame. She checked and reloaded the cylinders and twirled the gun like a man. The kid and Pilchuck dragged Burn's and Tragg's body over into a cluster of ground pine.

Squirrel-tooth Mary mounted Tragg's horse and they sent Burn's horse heading into a field. They mounted and rode west. By mid-afternoon they stopped on a hill and looked back. They saw a large black living mass moving steadily in their direction.

"How many?" the kid asked.

"I make it ta be more'n twenty," Pilchuck said. "Could be thirty."

"Let's ride," the stranger said.

They started out at a slow gait then hit it hard along the straight road. By late afternoon they stopped at a high point again to look back. The saw a spot of red in the distance. The posse had stopped to build a campfire.

"They stopped," the kid said. "That's good."

"Not all of them," Mary said. "They most likely sent spotters after us. We gotta keep on a goin'."

As exhausted as they and their horses were, they started off again. An hour on and it began to rain, slow at first, then heavy and hard. They had to slow down and watch the road in fear of losing it.

"The rain will wipe out our tracks," Mary said.

A few miles on Mary called a stop and pointed to the right, to a field. By then it stopped raining and twilight settled in. It was hard to see in the distance.

"Over there, to the right! I know a second way in ta Hell's Kitchen. Croak showed it ta me once. Nobody else knows of it!"

"Yer crazy!" Pilchuck yelled. "I'd a knowd about it! Croak woulda showed me!"

"Suit yerself, Pilchuck!"

Without another word, the pixie-like girl brushed the rain-soaked hair out of her blue eyes and rode off. The kid followed her, and the rest quickly fell in behind. They soon entered a stand of aspens. Beyond that they came upon a field. They cut through it into a tall forest of pine trees.

"Yer lost aincha!" Pilchuck yelled. "It's too dark to go on! Let's rest."

The girl ignored his taunt and kept going. It was getting darker and they could barely see her up ahead. After a while all they could do was follow the sound of her horse. The hours dragged on. It began to get lighter. Finally, up ahead, they saw the light of an opening. Moments later they came out into a grassy area and a small stream. They dismounted.

"We kin rest here," Mary said. "Thet posse ain't never gonna find us."

The sun came out and it got warmer. They unsaddled the horses and let them graze while they made camp. Using their saddles for a pillow, they spread their blankets and went to sleep.

The stranger was the first to wake. The sun was warm. He heard some water splashing and he looked and saw Squirrel-tooth Mary naked, taking a bath in the stream. He watched her. She ignored him. Finally she got dressed and came over and gave him a kiss on the cheek.

"Mornin' handsome." She was acting like an innocent little girl because it suited her. It seemed to be her way of charming people.

She went over to Pilchuck and nudged him awake. "Rise 'n shine, Pilchuck. We eat 'n go."

Pilchuck stood up. The kid came awake and sat rubbing his eyes.

"Who the hell put you in charge, girl?" Pilchuck said. He was in ill humor.

"Seein' as I'm the only one that knows where the hell we are, I guess I'm the ramrod, ain't I?"

"Well, I ain't takin' no orders from no back-stabbin', cheatin' tramp-slut," Pilchuck growled. "An' I'm a gonna tell Croak about you 'n thet Sprague, too. See ifn I don't, girl!"

"No you won't," Squirrel-tooth Mary said calmly.

"You gonna stop me?"

"Hell yes!" the girl said. "Draw, you sidewinder!"

Pilchuck drew quicker but his aim was off. His shot hit Squirrel-tooth Mary in her right side just as her shot hit him in the chest, knocking him flat on his backside. He fired again, missing. Her second shot hit him in the heart and he was slammed backwards. He lay there looking up at the sky.

The stranger rushed to the girl and lowered her gently to the ground. He held her in his arms and brushed the hair out of her eyes.

"Gosh," she said. "Look what I done, handsome?"

Her face was pale. She had trouble breathing.

The kid went to Pilchuck to see if he was alive.

"He's a gonner."

"Tear off his shirt, Wichita," the stranger said. "Hurry."

"The kid went to work getting Pilchuck's shirt. The stranger took it and tied it tight around the girl's waist, covering the wound.

"Thanks handsome," the girl said. She pulled his head down and kissed him on the mouth."

They lay her gently on the grass and saddled their horses. The stranger mounted the big outlaw stallion and held his arms out. Wichita lifted the girl up and the stranger hoisted her into the saddle in front. She lay back between his arms.

"Take me home," she whispered softly. Her pure blue eyes had a glazed, dull look in them. He knew she was dying.

The kid mounted up and they sat there looking around, now knowing which way to go.

"Which way, baby-doll?"

"Follow the eagles," Squirrel-tooth Mary said. She lifted a weak arm and pointed upward. He looked and saw where eagles dipped and rose, dipped and rose above distant pines.

The stranger led the way, moving slowly and gently, following an old, overgrown trail that led deep into the damp forest.

"You got a girl?" Mary asked. Her voice was so faint, that he could barely hear it.

"No," the stranger said.

"Why not?"

"I've been looking for one like you, beautiful."

"You gonna make an honest girl outta me?"

"As soon as we find a preacher," the stranger said.

"Do ya love me? Love me true?"

"Yes," the stranger whispered. "I love you true."

Squirrel-tooth Mary smiled. She fell quiet and limp in the stranger's arms, closing her blue eyes with a sigh.

13.

There was something tragic yet comical about old Croak Cantrell. He looked and acted like a relic from days gone by. His band of outlaws were never very successful. They never robbed any trains because he wasn't all that physical, being overweight. They did rob a lot of small town banks but never shot anybody unless they had to. That was the gentle side of him. In fact, they usually got the worst of any shoot out. But he never left a wounded or dead comrade behind.

After the Cheneyville Cattlemen's Association job, Croak Cantrell decided to retire. He found a place to build a secret roost where the law would never get to him. He called it Hell's Kitchen because the food was bad as hell. The Cheneyville robbery netted Croak Cantrell a cool half-million dollars in bank certificates and cash. He would never have to rob again.

Croak was a one-woman man, and that woman was Squirrel-tooth Mary. It was love at first sight. They were the complete physical opposites. He was big, broad, and stocky, and had a voice as course as gravel. In spite of her slight overbite, she was pretty, small, and fragile, with a voice like a songbird, and a smile that could melt any cowboy's heart.

They met one day by accident when she was trying to rob the same dinky town bank as he was, but by herself. His gang rode in to do the same job. She rode off with them and Croak and Squirrel-tooth Mary became as one.

One distinct difference between Mary and Croak was that he was dull witted and slow to move whereas she was impulsive and quick and did things on the spur of a moment. She was adventurous and had no fear or no sense of danger. It was this complete disregard for caution that landed her in the Bucknel County jail with one of Mallory Dunn's gang, an outlaw named Sprague. He convinced her that the bank in Hudnell was easy pickings. It wasn't.

So Croak Cantrell sat in his little log cabin and brooded. He drank heavily as he pondered the fate of his beloved Squirrel-tooth Mary. The rotgut whiskey was supposed to dull the pain, but the more he drank the worse he felt and the more he fretted.

"If he don't cut her loose he'll be one dead Judge," Croak said to one of the two men in the room at the table with him. He shook his head to clear the whiskey from his brain.

"Whatta ya mean by thet, Croak?" one asked.

"Well he's got my girl 'n I got two of his! Thet's what I mean!"

"Whatta ya thinkin' of doin' to 'em?"

"Kill 'em is what!"

"Both of 'em?"

"Darn tootin', both of 'em!" Croaked belched air. "I'll choke 'em both with my bare hands, I will!"

They heard an outlaw shouting out on the road.

"They're back!"

The two cowboys jumped up and rushed from the cabin. The big outlaw stiffened a moment then rose up on unsteady legs and lumbered outside into the late afternoon gloom. He blinked at what he saw.

The stranger had Squirrel-tooth Mary in his arms, holding her from falling to the ground. She hung limp as a dead rabbit.

"Take her Croak," the stranger said in an exhausted voice. "She wants only you, now."

"Oh, God!" Croak Cantrell bellowed as if wounded.

He stepped down into the road and wobbled over to the stranger. Brazos eased Mary's body down into Croak's waiting arms. The big man took her and held her as if she were a delicate piece of glass he was afraid to break.

"Who did it?" Croak growled, about to explode. Tears were streaming down his leathery face.

"The posse," the kid said.

The big outlaw looked around, dazed and lost. Finally he turned and carried Mary slowly into the cabin. His enormous frame shook with tremors of sobbing.

The stranger and the kid dismounted and went in after the outlaw. He sat in a chair with Mary in his arms, rocking her gently to and fro.

"Tell me about it," Croak said, sniffing back tears.

The stranger started. "Well, we broke her out. It was a clean break and then the posse got on our trail. They came on fast. Our horses were already tired from the long ride to

Bucknel." The stranger paused. "The posse cornered us about forty miles from Bucknel." He stopped.

"Go on," Croak said.

The stranger looked over at the kid. The kid took up the story. "The posse cornered us about forty miles east of Bucknel, so we had to make a stand and fight it out. Burns and Pilchuck told us to make a break for it. They said getting' her back to you was all that mattered. They insisted we go on."

"Them was good boys," Croak said. He sniffed again. "Damn good outlaws. Go on."

The stranger picked it up. "Well, we were fine that day and the next until Mary's horse went lame and slowed us down quite a bit. The posse caught up with us again. That's when Burns told the kid and me to keep going. He'd hold them off. Just as we rode away, Mary got winged. I grabbed her off her horse and we made a run for it. I saw Burns standing charging like a bull right into a hail of bullets with his guns blazing. The posse shot him all to hell."

"Yeah, that was Burnsy, alright. Loyal through and through."

"He did you proud, Croak," the kid said.

"We were lucky we got away. I guess God wanted us to get her back to you, Croak," the stranger said.

"Well at least they never got to hang my baby-doll."

"She's all yours now."

"Yeah, I guess so," the outlaw chief sobbed. Then, "I'd like ta be alone fer a while now, fellers."

"Sure Croak," the stranger said. He got up and stared down at Squirrel-tooth Mary. He reached down and brushed the hair out of her eyes. He stood staring at her a moment before he and the kid went outside.

They took their horses over to the stable and took off the saddles and rigs and turned them over to the attendant to be fed and washed down. After that they walked slowly over to the hotel.

"You think we shoulda told him what really happened?" the kid asked.

"He wouldn't have believed us," the stranger said. "It's best this way. We're all heroes and Mary is a legend." The kid nodded.

"She was sure some gal, wasn't she?"

"Yeah but she was bound to end up this way."

"She got to you, didn't she?" the kid said.

"Yes, she really did." The stranger sighed, "I'm tired as hell."

"Those stinking cots in the hotel will seem pretty nice after what we've been through."

"They sure will."

The next day they buried Squirrel-tooth Mary in the pine forest where there were over a dozen graves with crosses. An outlaw preacher read from a Bible. After the funeral the kid and the stranger spoke to Croak.

"What about the Judge's wife?"

"What about her?" the old outlaw didn't seem so very friendly any more.

"Let me and the kid get her out of here. That'll keep the posse from snooping around. They might get lucky. They could come in here and wipe this place out," the stranger said.

"Let me talk to Mallory Dunn first," Croak said. "See what he says."

"I thought you were the ramrod," the stranger said.

"I am, but maybe there's a chance for a big ransom."

"You don't want to get into that game, my friend. It ain't healthy."

"Yeah, maybe I should jest let the boys have some fun with 'em," Croak said. He seemed meaner and harder than he did before.

"You can't do that, Croak! There's the code!" the kid blurted out. "You go agin the code and yer fair game!"

"Well, I'll jest see what ol' Mallory has ta say."

"What about me and the kid?"

"What about it?"

"How about we leave?"

The old outlaw sniffed and looked away, avoiding their eyes. "Let me sleep on thet."

Suddenly the kid said, "Mr. Cantrell, sir, I'd like to meet Mr. Dunn. I really would like ta do thet."

"You would?"

"Yes, sir," the kid said eagerly, almost like a child wanting candy. "I really would."

"Why?"

"Well, I'd kinda like to kill him."

The outlaw started to laugh. It turned into a roar. Finally he simmered down.

"Are you serious, kid?"

"Yep. Like I said, I want ta kill Mr. Dunn."

Croak Cantrell snickered. "I wish somebody would. He's been a pure pain in my backside." Then, "Well, I could invite him to supper at the hotel tonight." He turned to the stranger. "Don't blame me, Brazos ifn you have to bury the kid. He'll be dead before the supper is over."

"I think he's got his mind set on dying," the stranger said.

Croak Cantrell lumbered away laughing.

The stranger and the kid went back to the hotel. They hadn't seen Mrs. Risdale and her daughter since they had left over a week ago. They knocked and were invited into the woman's room.

"You were gone a long time," Vera Risdale said. "How did your plan work out?"

"Not so good. We'll need another one."

Mrs. Risdale gave him a blank, unrevealing stare. "I have one."

"What is it?"

"I'll tell you this evening, Mr. Brazos. Better yet, I'll show you."

She spoke with confidence.

14.

That evening the stranger and the kid went down to the lobby. They stood there staring into the dining room. Vera Risdale and her daughter sat alone at a table in a far corner. A large table in the middle of the room caught their attention. Five men sat there. One was Croak Cantrell, and three were cowboy outlaws. The fifth man was a tall middle-aged man. He was Mallory Dunn. The kid recognized him from the posters he had seen.

"There's Dunn," the kid said through clenched teeth. His body started to shake. Dunn glanced towards them and then said something to the three cowboys. They all laughed.

"I guess Croak told him about you."

"Yeah, looks like it," the kid said. He didn't look too well.

"Relax, take a deep breath and smile," the stranger said. "Don't show them anything, kid." Then, "This is gonna be your night. I can feel it. Your stars are all lined up, kid."

The kid tried to smile but couldn't. He was scared.

The stranger stepped down into the rustic dining room and walked towards the buffet table. The kid was close on his heels. They got a steak, a boiled potato, some beans, and coffee. They dropped an eagle in the hat and sat at a table near the wall.

"I don't feel so good, Brazos," the kid muttered weakly. "I feel kinda strange."

"It'll pass," the stranger said.

Suddenly Mallory Dunn stood up and checked his gun, spinning the cylinder. The room went deadly quiet. Dunn shoved the gun back into its holder and picked up his coffee cup and took a long drink and put it down, all the time with his eyes on the kid. Finally he coughed and walked slowly towards the kid's table.

"Here he comes, kid," the stranger said. "Show the son of a bitch what you're made of."

"Oh, shit!" the kid said. "I ain't hungry no more. Let's go!"

"Too late, kid. Watch his eyes."

Mallory Dunn was all of six feet four inches tall. He had wide shoulders and his wavy hair was tinged with grey.

The kid turned to look into the face of death. Death had a wide mustache that covered its upper lip, and dimpled cheeks as it smiled down at him. Its eyes were coal-black and deep. Death came right up to the table and chuckled.

"Croak says you're lookin' fer me, kid," the voice of death said. Death reached down and picked up the kids cup of coffee, spit in it, and put it slowly down.

The kid slowly stood up, his eyes fastened on Mallory Dunn's face.

"Yes, sir, Mr. Dunn," the kid said. His voice was barely above a whisper. His legs suddenly stopped shaking.

The kid slowly dropped his gun hand down low. Dunn didn't notice. He was too busy glancing over at Vera Risdale who had coughed to get his attention. He saw her and smiled. She smiled back and nodded at him. He was a very big, important man and was about to put on a free show of gunmanship.

Dunn finally looked back at the kid and chuckled.

"Okay, kid, who was it? Who did I kill? Your dad? Your girlfriend? Your cat or dog?" Deaths voice was clear and it spoke as if it had learning. "Who? What? Speak up, kid!"

The kid looked down at his coffee cup a moment, as if to make sure where it was.

"You killed my daddy, Mr. Dunn," the kid growled.

"Is that all?" Death chuckled smugly, as if amused.

"And you raped and killed my mommy." The kid's voice was a little louder and firmer.

Dunn stepped back a step.

"And my little sister!" The kid's voice rang out with rage and echoed about the room. Everyone heard it.

Suddenly Mallory Dunn didn't look like Death anymore. He had an uncertain look on his face.

Mallory Dunn went for his gun.

The kid knew it was coming. He saw the telltale narrowing of Dunn's eyes. The kid's hand brought the coffee cup up swiftly and it smacked Dunn in the jaw. Hot coffee covered the outlaw's face. He flinched and fired but the kid leaned sideways to the right. Dunn's bullet blew a hole in the pinewood wall near the kid's head.

The kid fired off three quick snap-shots. One bullet hit Dunn in the belly, one hit him center chest, and the third hit him between the eyes. Dunn toppled forward like a cut-down tree. His face hit the tabled and bounced off, as his body fell to the floor.

'Oh my God!" someone yelled. "I don't believe it!"

Croak Cantrell and the three cowboy outlaws came over to look at Dunn's body. The old outlaw nudged it. He chuckled. "Yep! Dunn's bought the farm, boys. Best git him outta here before he starts collectin' flies."

Dunn's men looked at the kid and the stranger and decided they didn't want to pursue the matter. They picked Dunn up and took him away.

The kid wasn't responding to all the attention. He looked like he was going to be sick.

"Best take the kid into the bar," Croak said. "He needs a drink of rot gut real quick. It's on the house."

The stranger took the kid by the arm and let him away. Vera Risdale and her daughter smiled at them as they went out.

The kid and the stranger went through the lobby to the bar. Croak followed. "Give the kid anything he wants," Croak said and left.

"Two rot guts," the stranger said. He let the kid drink them both. They got a bottle and sat at a table.

The kid shook his head to clear it. "What did I just do?"

"You put three air-holes in Mallory Dunn, kid. One for your father, mother, and your little sister, I guess."

"I did?"

"Yeah, you gave him lead poisoning, alright."

"I did?"

"You don't remember?"

"All I remember is he made me so darn mad I saw red."

"Well, he won't do that again, Wichita." Brazos said with a chuckle.

Suddenly they saw Vera Risdale and Grace staring at them from the lobby. Vera walked away but Grace stood there a moment longer, alone, staring at the kid, then left.

"She sure is purdy," the kid said.

"Yeah and so is her mother," the stranger said.

"Let's git stinkin' drunk," the kid said.

"Sure, why not?" Brazos said. But he left the drinking to the kid.

Someone had to stay alert.

15.

"Seems like a waste, if ya ask me, Croak," one of the outlaws said. "Maybe we could have some fun with 'em before lettin' 'em go."

"Yeah," the other one said. "Those two stuck-up bitches need to be broken in proper like. They ain't had the taste of a real cowboy yet."

Croak Cantrell stared at the flickering shadows on the wall made by the sputtering oil lamp above the table. He seemed to be deep in thought. There was sadness in his eyes. He sighed. He missed his baby-doll. She was gone forever now.

"Alright, whatever you guys say."

He rose up slowly from his chair looking defeated and weary. He had nothing to live for now that Mary was gone. She had been his lynchpin for these past years. Now there was nothing but emptiness left in a big heart where love once lived. Life was dull without her smiling face, her musical laughter. Croak was a one-woman man.

Across the lake, the Hell's Kitchen dining room was dark and empty and the bar was starting to close for the night. A single oil lamp shone in the lobby, on the reception desk.

Upstairs in their room, Vera Risdale and her daughter sat on the bed staring at the closed door. They were fully dressed. An oil lamp sat on the stand by the washbowl.

"We shouldn't wait any longer, mother," Grace said.

Vera Risdale nodded. She stood up. "I'll go do it. Be ready to go."

"I will, but hurry. They are our only hope, mother."

Vera Risdale quickly left, closing the door behind her. She hurried across the hall to the stranger's room and knocked.

"Mr. Brazos!" She said it twice before he answered the door with a gun in his hand. He waved her in. She saw the kid asleep on his cot in his clothes.

"What is it?" the stranger asked.

"Do you have a moment?"

"Why yes, ma'am."

She stood close, looking up into his eyes.

"We have to leave here tonight," Vera Risdale said. "I have a feeling something horrible is going to happen to me and my daughter." There was concern, almost panic, in her voice. She put a hand on his arm and gripped it tightly.

"But you don't know for sure," he said.

"No, but I can feel it coming. Please believe me!"

"You think he'll hurt you?"

"Worse than that."

The stranger went over to the table and offered her a chair. "Would you like to sit? We can talk."

She didn't move. "Didn't you hear what I just said, Mr. Brazos? I'm in a dire situation!"

"Look, ma'am, I just don't see how I can get us out of here right this minute, tonight. I'll need more time."

"There isn't going to be any time, sir!" Her voice was urgent.

"Ma'am, there's probably a hundred or more bad guys out there looking for a chance to take me and the kid down.

Those are not good odds, ma'am," the stranger explained softly. "We'll need help."

"I'll help you," Vera Risdale said forcefully.

The stranger chuckled. "You'll help me, ma'am? How?"

Vera Risdale walked over to the washstand, picked up the oil lamp and threw it hard at the wall. It burst and shattered, spewing oil. The wall exploded in flames.

"You'd better come with me," the woman said calmly. She went out the door.

The stranger grabbed his gun belt. The kid sat up and rubbed his eyes. He seemed in a daze.

"We're leaving kid," Brazos said.

"My head hurts."

Men's voices sounded in the hallway. The stranger looked out and saw Croak Cantrell with two outlaws at the top of the stairs. Mrs. Risdale was just about to go into her room.

"Hi, ma'am," Croak said drunkenly just as the stranger and the kid came out with their guns on.

"Hi, Croak," the stranger said. "What's up?"

Croak cleared his throat. "I'm a takin' Mrs. Risdale here an' her daughter to a shin-dig. Ain't I ma'am?"

Vera Risdale looked angry for a second then smiled a big, happy smile. "Well, of course you are, sir! Let me see if my daughter is ready. I shan't be but a moment, sir."

"Sure, ma'am." Croak said. He was unsteady on his feet. "Go git her, ma'am."

Grace Risdale opened the door. Her mother quickly stepped inside and shut it.

Suddenly one of the outlaws pointed to flames shooting out of the door to the stranger's room. "Holy cow! Their room is on fire, Croak!"

Just then they heard glass shatter in the Risdale room. Vera and Grace came out.

"I'm afraid our room is on fire, too," Vera said. Orange, crackling flames lit up their room. It crawled into the hallway.

The two outlaws turned and ran down the stairs.

Croak Cantrell stood swaying drunkenly on rubbery legs, trying to make sense of what was happening. The kid and the stranger walked up to him.

"Let's go get the fire brigade, Croak," the stranger said. He and the kid both grabbed an arm and led the big man down the stairs. Vera and Grace followed. The two outlaws were standing at the bottom with guns drawn. They seemed as drunk as Croak was.

"Say the word, Croak, and we'll plug 'em!"

"He's got a gun in my back, an' the hotel is burnin' down! Go git the fire brigade, you idjits!" They ran out into the night.

Using the old outlaw as a shield, they made their way around the lake towards the stables.

The air was beginning to turn orange behind them as the hotel, built of pine logs, went up in flames. They could hear the dry wood exploding. Flames leapt skyward as the inferno spread from room to room and down to the lower floor.

"What's next?" the stranger asked Mrs. Risdale.

"We're getting out of here just like we came in, on the stagecoach, Mr. Brazos. Do you think you can handle that part?"

"I do indeed, ma'am."

"Fine. It's all in your hands, now."

Outlaws were rushing out of their cabins and running towards the lake to join the fire brigade. Croak watched through foggy eyes, not resisting.

In half an hour they were at the stables. The stagecoach was there, intact and untouched. The stranger pulled Croak's gun from its holster and gave it to Mrs. Risdale.

"Shoot him in the belly if he moves."

"With pleasure," she said, smiling.

The stranger and the kid started hitching up the horses. There was just enough light from the fire and the moon above to work by. They saddled two extra horses and tied them to the rear of the coach.

"You'll never get out of here alive." Croak said, finally deciding to talk. "They'll shoot ya all to ribbons at the chokepoint."

"No they won't," the stranger said.

"Oh, how's thet?"

"Because you'll be up front driving and I'll have a gun in your fat gut," the stranger said.

Suddenly the big man sighed. "Looky here, I was a thinkin' maybe it is best fer you all to vamoose outta here anyhow." He sniffed and wiped his big nose. "Shucks, now thet Mallory Dunn is outta tha way, well, things will git back ta tha way they was before, an' all."

"You're lying!" Mrs. Risdale pressed the barrel of the gun hard against the outlaw's belly.

"No, no, ma'am! Old Croak ain't a lyin'. Now thet my baby-doll is, well you know, gone, there ain't no reason to hold none o' you no more."

"So, what do you propose, sir?" Vera asked.

"Well, I figure I could get you all past the chokepoint an' I could come back here. You all could jest keep a goin' on yer own then, okay?"

Grace Risdale said, "I don't trust him, mother. He's too tricky. A while ago he was going to give us over to his men."

"Naw! Old Croak wus jest pretendin', ma'am," the outlaw chief said. "I wouldn't a done thet, little lady. Ol' Croak knows the code, he does."

Suddenly the stranger said, "Time to go! In the coach, ladies!" The kid and the women got in the stagecoach. "Okay, Croak, up on top!"

"Take it easy, Brazos? I ain't no spring chicken!"

The stranger prodded the old outlaw up onto the driver's bench and got alongside him. He held the barrel of his Colt against his ribs.

"Just play it straight, old timer."

"Shucks," the outlaw said. "I said I'd git ya all outta here, didn't I? Croak Cantrell never goes back on his word."

The big man snapped the reins and spoke softly to the team of two horses. They moved slowly and the coach headed out onto the road and around the lake. No one saw them. Everyone seemed to be either at the lake or at the fire.

16.

The road out of Hell's Kitchen wound past the graveyard and into the pine trees. The old outlaw stopped the stagecoach a moment and stared. Squirrel-tooth Mary's grave stood higher than the rest, on a small knoll.

"Be seein' ya soon, baby-doll," the outlaw said under his breath, and snapped the reins. The road, from there on, slanted steeply upward until it came to where the higher surrounding cliffs closed together to form a narrow opening called a chokepoint.

There was a guard shack there by the entrance. It was lit by an oil lamp.

Just as they approached, a short, stocky outlaw came out on Croak's side of the coach. He had a rifle. Croak pulled back on the reins and put on the brakes to keep the coach from rolling backwards.

"It's me, Croak!"

The guard stood staring hard, trying to make out who was on the bench next to his boss.

Another taller guard came out from the shack with his rifle.

"Hi, boss!" the tall outlaw said, yawning. Suddenly he looked back down into the valley. "Say, what's thet down there, boss? Looks like the town is on fire!"

Croak laughed nervously.

"It's jest the hotel," the outlaw chief said. "But the fire brigade is got it under control."

"Where you goin' this hour a night, boss?" the short outlaw asked. "How come you ain't down there taking charge?"

"Brazos an' me, we're a takin' the ladies ta Bucknel," Croak said. "We're done with 'em. Don't need 'em anymore."

"Now? This time a night? With tha town afire? Thet don't sound right, Croak" the tall outlaw said.

The short outlaw made a move to open the stagecoach door. He was met by a blast of gunfire that knocked him flat on the road.

Croak Cantrell snapped the reins hard and yelled. The team bolted forward just as the tall outlaw snapped off a shot with his Winchester. Before he could lever in another round the kid reached out of the coach and winged him.

The stagecoach went hurtling through the moonlit pine forest for about five miles before it came to a stop. The old outlaw dropped the reins, slumped side-ways and fell to the ground. The stranger got down quickly and knelt beside him.

"I got back-shot," the outlaw gasped. "By my own man. Now that's a laugh fer ya, ain't it?" He coughed.

The kid jumped out of the coach and rushed over. "Mr. Cantrell, are you hurt bad?"

"Yeah, kid. I'm a dyin' 'n that's fer sure."

Vera Risdale stepped out of the coach and came over to the dying man. He stared up at her and smiled. She reached down and took his huge hand in both of hers.

"Is thet you, baby-doll?" he asked.

"No, Mr. Cantrell, it's me Vera Risdale."

"Oh, for a minute thar I thought…" His voice trailed off and his body went slack. Mrs. Risdale gentle placed his hand down on his chest. She got back into the coach.

The stranger got a shovel out of the coach toolbox and found a soft spot under the pines. He began digging. The winds whispered high in the pine branches. A lone owl sat watching from a nearby scrub oak. Every few minutes it let out a whooo-whooo.

"He wasn't such a bad old fart," the kid said, as he dug.

"His is a dying breed, Wichita," the stranger said. "He was the last of the gentle ones."

"He wasn't like Mallory Dunn, that's fer sure."

"Yeah, Dunn gave all outlaws a bad name."

The left the grave unmarked. In a year it would be grown over by weeds and nobody would ever know that Croak Cantrell was pushing up wildflowers there.

They mounted back up with the kid driving the team. The horses seemed to know the way out so he let them chose the path. In two more hours they were on the post road. They headed west towards Bucknel. The kid looked back but couldn't see where they had come out of Hell's Kitchen. None of them would every find the way in again.

About forty miles east of Bucknel they came up on a stage layover. It was daylight by then. The kid drove the stagecoach up under the shade of a stand of trees, out of the sun. They all got down and stretched and yawned.

"Just go in there and tell the station manager who you are, Mrs. Risdale," the stranger said. "He'll take care of you and your daughter." The kid was staring at Grace Risdale. She stared back.

Vera Risdale stood close to the stranger. "I want to give you your reward, Mr. Brazos," she said. She took his face between her hands and kissed him. "If you every come to Bucknel." She let it go at that.

The stranger chuckled. "I just might do that, some night, that is, ma'am."

"I shall be eagerly awaiting your visit, sir."

"Well, Miss Grace," the kid said. "I guess you can't wait ta get back home?"

"Where will you go, Wichita?" Grace asked.

"A further ways west, I reckon," the kid said. "I'm gonna get me a little farm, like my mommy and daddy had."

"Oh, really?" It was clear by the tone of her voice that Grace Risdale was never going to be a farmer's wife.

There was an awkward silence. The women looked anxiously towards the station house. The stranger nodded and untied the two horse from the rear of the coach. He and the kid mounted up and tipped their hats.

"Good-bye, ma'am," the stranger said.

They nodded and walked their horses out on the post road. They stopped there, looking at each other.

"How did you figure Dunn out, kid?" the stranger asked.

"You told me how. You said look at his eyes. When I saw them squint, I knew it was a comin' my way."

"Where'd you learn that coffee cup trick?"

The kid chuckled. "I read thet in a penny dreadful."

They both laughed.

Suddenly the stranger looked serious. "Look, kid, you gotta be careful now. You'll be known as the one that out drew Mallory Dunn. You did the law a favor, but every gunny in the territory will be coming to call you out."

The kid nodded. "Yeah, I know."

There didn't seem to be much more to say. They shook hands and the kid rode west. The stranger rode east.

They didn't see Vera and Grace Risdale watching them from the station yard, waving their final good-bye. Both women watched until the cowboys were out of sight and then walked slowly over to the station house.

A sudden warm wind caught at their dresses and pulled on their bonnets, as if sorry to see them leave. They looked back at the post road. It was empty.

Vera and Grace Risdale finally went into the station house. It was time to go home.

The End.

About the Author

R. Annan is a seasoned and traveled author with many interests. As a career serviceman he served in Korea and Vietnam. He also completed a one-year course at the Defense Language Institute at Monterey, California, and graduated from the University of South Florida with a B.A. in Art and Art History. After taking a two-year course in screenwriting at the Hollywood Scriptwriting Institute, he established *The Old Time Radio Club Time Machine* as both a scriptwriter and an actor.

A Note from the Author

Thank you for reading my book. If you enjoyed it, would you please consider rating and reviewing it? I'd enjoy your feedback. Here is a link to my author's page on Amazon: www.amazon.com/author/rannan

Look for other books to appear soon. Thank you!